# Little Workmates

# Vet Vicky

by Mandy Ross

illustrated by Emma Dodd

**Ladybird**

Vet Vicky drove to work as usual in her blue vet van. When she arrived at the surgery, there was already a noisy queue waiting.

"What a lot of poorly pets this morning!" said Vicky.

This is Vet Vicky. She looks after all of Story Town's animals, large and small.

A catalogue record for this book is available from the British Library

Published by Ladybird Books Ltd
80 Strand  London  WC2R 0RL
A Penguin Company

2 4 6 8 10 9 7 5 3 1

© LADYBIRD BOOKS LTD MMIV

Illustrations © Emma Dodd MMIV

LADYBIRD and the device of a Ladybird are trademarks of Ladybird Books Ltd

"Barker's very quiet," said Mrs Dogsberry. "He's lost his bark."

Vet Vicky checked Barker over. She gave Mrs Dogsberry some doggy tablets to put in Barker's dinner.

"Don't worry, he'll soon be barking again," she said.

DOG

"Tibbles fell from a branch and hurt his leg," said Fireman Fergus.

Vet Vicky checked Tibbles over. She bandaged his poorly leg.

"Don't worry, he'll soon be climbing trees again," she said.

"My mouse isn't moving at all," said Builder Bill. "I think she's..."

EEK! Suddenly, the mouse leapt out of his hands.

"Hmmm," said Vet Vicky. "That mouse looks fine to me!"

At last, Vet Vicky had helped all the poorly pets.

"Time to go to Farmer Fred's," she said. "Daisy the cow hasn't been eating her food."

But when Vicky arrived at the farm...

"Daisy's gone!" said Farmer Fred, in a flap. "She was in the field earlier. She must have got out through a gap in the fence!"

"Don't worry, Farmer Fred," said Vet Vicky. "We'll find her. Now where would a runaway cow want to go?" she wondered.

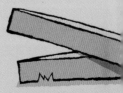

While Farmer Fred mended the fence, Vet Vicky looked outside the field. She noticed some hoof-prints along the lane. Vicky followed the hoof-prints until...

"Shoo! Shoo!" she heard someone shouting. It was Teacher Tina.

"Oh, no!" cried Vet Vicky. There was Daisy, happily munching the flowers in the school garden.

Vet Vicky made a sign to the children to be quiet. Then she crept up quietly behind Daisy and slipped a rope around the cow's neck.

"Moooooo!" mooed Daisy.

"Well, Daisy," whispered Vicky. "You seem to be eating again."

Teacher Tina and the children waved as Vet Vicky led Daisy out of the school.

"Children, make sure you don't step under Daisy's hooves," said Teacher Tina.

And no one did.

Back at the farm, Vet Vicky checked Daisy over.

"Daisy is a very healthy cow," she said. "Maybe she just needs some more flowers, as a treat, now and then."

"Moooooo!" nodded Daisy.

Farmer Fred gave Vet Vicky a fat round cheese, made from Daisy's milk.

"Thank you, Vet Vicky," he said. "We'll make sure Daisy has plenty of flowers to eat from now on!"

Footballer Fabio

Vet Vicky

Doctor Daisy

Builder Bill

Postman Pete

Fireman Fergus

Nurse Nancy